Max Rhymes™

A Children's Series

Be Responsible Like Max

Teaching core values, creating higher self-esteem and
increasing reading retention, all through the power of rhymes.

Todd & Jackie Courtney

Be Responsible Like Max
Max Rhymes™

Illustration and Copyright © 2018 by Inspired Imaginations, LLC

ISBN: 978-1-945200-23-6

Library of Congress Control Number: 2017919831

Published by:
Inspired Imaginations, LLC

Websites

MaxRhymes.com   MaxRhymesClub.com   MaxRhymesFoundation.org

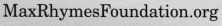

Words to Know
A Pre-Reading Activity

BROOM a brush that has a long handle and that is used for sweeping floors.

CARPET a heavy fabric cover for a floor.

CLEAN free from dirt, marks etc.; not dirty.

ORGANIZE to arrange and plan (an event or activity).

PERSONAL belonging or relating to a particular person.

POLITE having or showing good manners or respect for other people.

RULE a statement that tells you what is or is not allowed in a particular game, situation, etc.

VACUUM CLEANER an electrical machine that cleans floors, rugs, etc., by sucking up dirt, dust, etc.

After I wake up
and hop onto the floor,
I always make my bed
before I walk out the door.

I need to get myself dressed
before it's time to go to school.
No one should do it for me,
that is my personal rule.

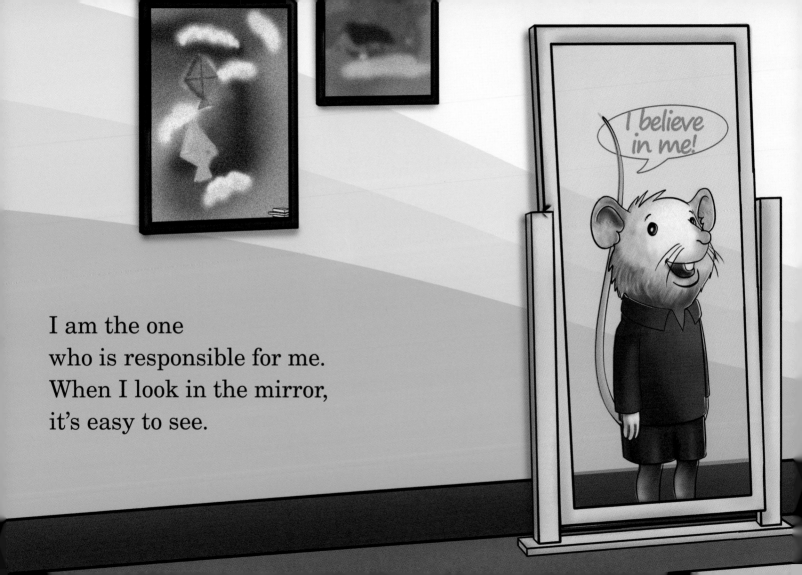

I am the one
who is responsible for me.
When I look in the mirror,
it's easy to see.

I always pick up my toys
and make sure things are put away.
These are my responsibilities
because I was the one who played.

It's my responsibility
to do what I think is right.
No one should have to tell me,
it's not nice to get into a fight.

It's my responsibility
to always clean my room.
I use the vacuum on the carpet,
because it won't clean with a broom.

Helping Mommy with the dishes
is the polite thing to do.
We eat together as a family,
so we clean together
when we are through.

Here you go, Mommy.

I should always brush my teeth every morning and every night. It's my job to keep my teeth clean, and to make sure I do it right.

I always take time to organize
before I go to bed.
I get my backpack together,
and make sure my book was thoroughly read.

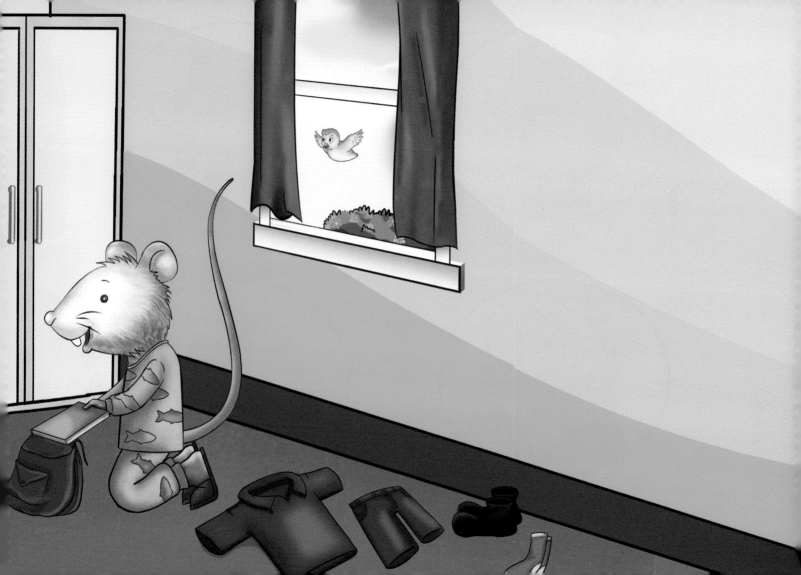

Mama

Papa

Max

Molly

Rosie

Kenny

Stella

Ricky

Did you find Max's hidden books?

SYNOPSIS

Be Responsible Like Max is a collection of rhymes that focus on inspiring children to be responsible for themselves by making their beds, cleaning up their toys, clearing the table, and more. Each rhyme affirms a belief that will develop a sense of ownership from their actions, accountability, self-care, and an awareness of others.

THEME

Be Responsible Like Max is ideal for teaching children that being responsible means being dependable, telling the truth, accepting the consequences for what they do or say. Responsible people treat everyone with kindness and respect. Teaching responsibility is building up a routine and "I Believe in Me" will soon become their main mantra!

PARENT IDEAS

After reading, Be Responsible Like Max, ask a few questions.

- How was Max responsible when he woke up in the morning?
- Who got Max dressed for school?
- After Max and Molly played with their toys, who picked up?
- How was Max responsible after eating?

We each have responsibilities to ourselves and to others. Responsible children try to do their best. When they make a mistake, they don't blame others. They demonstrate personal responsibility by owning their mistake.

Reread the rhyme:

"It's my responsibility to do what I think is right. No one should have to tell me, it's not nice to get into a fight."

Show the picture to your child.
- What is happening in this picture?
- How is Rosie feeling?
- What did Max do to make the situation better?

What responsibilities do I have to myself, my family, my school, my community and my world?

We each have a responsibility to ourselves and to others. Responsible people try to do their best.

When responsible people make mistakes, they don't blame others. They take personal responsibility for their actions.

Create your own responsible choice checklist!

RESPONSIBLE CHOICE CHECKLIST

10 Responsible Habits of Successful Children

Examples:
- I always tell the truth, even when I might get into trouble.
- I do my best work EVERY day.
- I share and make sure everyone gets a turn.

Max Rhymes™ Books

A Children's Series

Be Responsible Like Max

Get Inspired with Max

Giving Thanks with Max

Max Gives Thanks to God

Max & Molly Learn Their Manners

Daydream with Max & Molly

The Science Behind Our Rhymes

Did you know questions:

- Did you know that 95% of our behavioral patterns are established by the age of 7?
- Did you know that babies recognize words, sounds and feelings while in the womb?
- Did you know that due to brain waves changes at such early stages in life, science tells us we should begin teaching our babies in utero?
- Did you know that the science of epigenetics has proven that our thoughts can modify our gene expression?
- Did you know that only 1 out of 10 adults ever change their behavioral patterns for the better, which confirms what science is telling us? That is, we should be teaching our infants and toddlers the positive virtues we want them to have in life prior to age 7.

Let's talk about brain waves!

A baby is born in a delta brain wave frequency. This is the lowest frequency and is the reason why their brains are like little sponges. Around age 2, the brain changes into a theta frequency which is still a low frequency, but higher than delta. This just means the brain will be a little less spongy than the delta frequency. However, around age 7, we move into an alpha frequency, which is a much higher frequency, and makes us less susceptible to learn so easily. In essence, it's kind of like being on auto pilot from age 7. Sounds scary, doesn't it? Around age 12 we move into a beta frequency, which is even higher, and the reason so many teenagers have a tough time learning things such as foreign languages. So, why is this important to know? Because it provides the science to back up why it's imperative to teach our infants and toddlers positive virtues prior to them reaching the age of 7.

What makes Max Rhymes different?

Due to early brainwave changes, science has proven the learning stage between ages 0–7 is one of the most important of our lives. Max Rhymes takes advantage of this learning period by teaching core values, creating a positive belief system, increasing reading retention and creating higher self-esteem, all through the power of rhymes.

Want to learn about epigenetics?

Keep reading!

Epigenetics:

the study of changes in organisms caused by modification of gene expression rather than alteration of the genetic code itself.

What does that mean to you as a parent?

It means you have a lot more influence on your child than we ever knew. Did you know that you have an impact on your child's IQ? Did you know that you have an impact on your child even before conception? Most of us didn't and still don't know this. However, research is revealing what others, such as aboriginal cultures, have known for 1000 years and it's why those cultures go through a ceremony to purify their minds and bodies.

Research is showing that parents, by default, act as genetic engineers months before conception. During the final stages of egg and sperm maturation, a process called genomic imprinting adjusts the activity of specific groups of genes that will shape the characteristics of the child yet to be conceived. (The Biology of Belief, Bruce Lipton; Surani 2001; Reik and Walter 2001) What that means is your stress levels, be it financial, relationship, family, friends, work, etc. and likewise your level of happiness and peacefulness, all play a role in the development of your child even before conception.

Now, on top of that, add the fact that **95% of the programming to the subconscious mind is done by the age of 7**. That means all the things your child has heard via conversations, TV or radio, is all getting programmed in the mind. It's this programming that plays a huge role in the child's future based on the "truths" and "beliefs" the child has been programmed with. Unfortunately, most of us have been programmed with limitations, which has prevented us from creating the life we deserve.

Endorsed By

"*Language acquisition plays a fundamental role in exercising an infant's brain and shaping its intelligence. Research reveals that interactive social experiences with parents, through conversation and reading, provides a gateway to enhancing a child's linguistic, cognitive, and emotional development.*

The social programming a child receives before age seven is the primary determinant of its health and fate as an adult. I encourage parents, grandparents and extended family members to review the new series of Max Rhymes by Todd and Jackie Courtney. Their compilations of beautifully illustrated, consciousness-enhancing messages are designed to elicit a child's intelligence, integrity, and respect for others and our planet. Max Rhymes is a powerful tool to help children reach their full potential…a benefit for all of humanity, since a child's behavior will ultimately influence the evolution of us all."

–Bruce H. Lipton, Ph.D.
Cell biologist, Specialist in Epigenetics, and
best-selling author of *The Biology of Belief*

About the Authors

Jacqueline "Jackie" Courtney, was born and raised in San Jose, CA. and has spent most of her life as an elementary school teacher in the grades of kindergarten through 3rd. With her talents as a teacher and private tutor, specializing in the area of reading, it was a natural for Jackie to follow her passion in the creation of children's books.

Todd J. Courtney was raised in San Jose, CA for most of his life. He has spent the past 29 years as a business owner and during the last 5 years, he was teaching what Wallace D. Wattles calls "thinking stuff" to business groups. As a devoted study on behavioral science and thought-provoking philosophy, he authored, *Thinking In One Direction,* which targets teens and young adults. To expand on the books philosophy, he created www.TeensCanDream.org; a site dedicated to help teens during those tumultuous years. He then created an animation video for children with leukemia called, *Just Imagine If…You were leukemia free!* www.JustImagineIf.org. Thereafter, he co-authored, with his wife Jackie, *Max Rhymes,* a children's book series with the purpose of bringing core values back into the mainstream. He is the founder of the Max Rhymes Foundation.